PAUL BUNYAN

by
Nanci A. Lyman

illustrated by
Bert Dodson

Folk Tales of America

Troll Associates

PROLOGUE

Probably no American folk hero is as famous as Paul Bunyan. According to all the stories told about him, he was the biggest and the best at *anything*. He also practically "built" the United States single-handedly, causing such familiar sights as the Rocky Mountains and the Mississippi River.

Well, no one believes *everything* about Paul Bunyan. But you can believe in his spirit and his courage and his determination to succeed. These things were part of all the brave men and women who helped to build and tame a young, wild country.

Library of Congress # 79-66320
ISBN 0-89375-310-6/0-89375-309-2 (pb)

E
L

(

ST. JOHN'S LUTHERAN
ELEMENTARY SCHOOL
"For a Christ-Centered Education"
3521 Linda Vista Ave.
Napa, California

Paul Bunyan was a logging man who never had an equal. Right from the beginning, he knew what he would be—a lumberjack!

Paul was born and raised near a logging camp. As soon as he could crawl, he found his way to the camp to listen to the men talk and watch them swing their axes. Lands had to be prepared to build towns, to clear fields for farming, to gather lumber for the hundreds of things a growing country needs. Then and there Paul made up his mind. The life of a lumberjack was all he would ever want. It was an excellent choice, too, for the young country was rich with forests.

No one is sure where Paul was born. Many stories of his life have been told. But if the truth be known, some of them simply must be doubted. More than one of the tales got their start from the loggers, who would sit around their campfires in the evenings. They'd laugh and tell of the day's events and of times past. It was only natural that a little exaggeration slipped in here and there.

In any event, it seems likely that Paul was born in Maine, maybe Canada—but probably Maine. People from Maine tell how their forefathers worried when baby Paul rolled in his crib, for often just a little toss could knock down a mile of trees. What might happen when he grew bigger and stronger! There was no need to fret, though, for being a natural-born logger, he had love and respect for his magnificent surroundings. He hardly ever took a misstep, seldom had an accident, and he always thought carefully about every move he made.

As you've probably guessed by now, Paul was one extraordinarily large fellow, by any standards. At birth, he weighed eighty-six pounds, give or take a few. When he was a

youngster, he quite naturally ate enormous amounts of food. One day, it is said, he ate seventy-four buckets of oatmeal and drank fourteen gallons of milk.

There were other "growing-pain" problems for Paul. For one thing, there was the matter of clothes. He kept growing so quickly in every direction that his mother had to make changes in his pants almost every week. And until his feet stopped growing, he didn't wear shoes. Imagine what a task that would have been, making new boots every few days! For some time, it's been said, Paul simply wore sheets for socks and kegs for shoes.

When he finally reached his full size, Paul was of majestic proportions. Early settlers in America used to refer to themselves as "wee people," because they claimed they came up only to Paul's ankles. Others will tell of his being taller than all but the highest of the pines. But, more likely, he was somewhere in-between. According to a good source, when Paul sat down, he needed fifty tree stumps to sit on. That's how big he was!

Maybe, maybe not. In any event, Paul made quite an impression. Usually he was seen in a red hunting cap, a mackinaw of orange and purple checks, gray and tan pants, and green socks.

Another problem that beset Paul when he was young was the matter of proper schooling. As it happened, he missed a lot of early training due to a typical childhood illness—the mumps! Paul never did anything in a small

way, so he had no ordinary case of the mumps. A host of doctors came to his home to cure him, but unfortunately about eleven years passed before Paul was able to get to the schoolhouse.

His schooling didn't go well either, although he would tell his parents, "I'm trying very hard."

The main things Paul had to concentrate on were reading, writing, and figures—and some geography. Right off, writing was a difficulty. Every time he wrote his name, he wore out a pencil. And he never did master the art of getting the curlicues on numbers just right.

There was a rumor that sometimes Paul was a bit unruly. But that doesn't seem very likely. Paul realized he was a bit big for his age and that he had a booming voice. So he tried very hard to speak softly, and tried not to cause undue disturbance. But even so, the girls were afraid of him, and he never had a chance to carry their books. The boys were afraid as well, for they could plainly see how powerful he was, and they would not fight him. Schooling simply didn't seem to be in Paul's plans.

But his mother and father were helpful. From his mother, he learned quite a bit about reading and writing. From his father, he learned a lot about figures and lumbering and farming. And from Mother Nature he learned everything he would ever need to know about the outdoors, which, after all, was to play the biggest role in his life. Besides, Paul himself was a most inventive fellow. He was always solving tricky problems. And this led to many of the machines and ways of building and figuring that we use today.

As happens to many young people, there came the day when, although still very young, he felt the need to leave his parents' farm to seek his own way—which, of course, had to be logging.

"I have to seek my fortune," he told his parents.

Paul's father, disappointed as he may have been, understood. He gave him a bit of money, some worthwhile advice, and his first pair of shoes. Paul's adventures were about to start.

Since logging was his calling, he quite properly found himself a good logging camp to join. Paul was given some lumber-cutting work, but because he was a newcomer, he was given other chores as well.

One job, it has been said, was that of a day-breaker. The cook would send Paul up into a mountain with an axe to break day. Paul was so quick he could always get his job done and get back to camp to call the men to breakfast long before daylight got there. He was also required to blow the dinner horn for the cook.

18

As time passed, Paul grew stronger and faster. He quickly learned how to square a tree, which a logger has to know. "Squaring a tree" is tricky. First the bark comes off. Then most loggers have to hack and hack until they get a log with four even sides. But not so with Paul. He could do it with just four cuts—one on each side of the tree, and the job was done.

After working about thirty minutes or thereabouts, he would have approximately one-third of an acre of trees all upright and clean. Then came the swing that made Paul famous. With one swing of his special axe, they'd all come down! Remarkable? Yes, but it was so.

Paul's axe was most unusual. He was always trying to improve his logging techniques, and his axe was one of his better inventions.

His regular axe had a handle made of a whole hickory tree. Now, normally, that would have been a fine tool, but he found that it broke whenever he had some especially fast chopping to do. So Paul thought the situation over for a spell, then nodded his head.

"I think I've got the answer," he muttered to himself.

Then he wove a rope, about fifty feet long, out of tall grass. On one end he made two holds for both his hands. On the other end he attached an enormous blade. Now for the test. He whirled the axe around him in a wide circle and found that he was able to cut down twenty trees with one stroke. Such a triumph! Others laughed at the strange axe, but they didn't laugh at what Paul did with it.

At last it was time for Paul to move on. He had learned all there was to know about logging. He could log better than anyone else. What would the next step be? It was a big step, so Paul decided to take some time off to think out his next move.

He was lonely. For some time he had been
swinging his axe and yelling *"Timber!"* Then,
all by himself, he would bundle the trees and
carry them under his arms to a river so they
could float to a sawmill. Sometimes he wished
he had a strong friend to help him. "I'm
lonely, there is no doubt," Paul said. "Maybe if
I had a friend my size . . ."

And then came the Winter of the Blue Snow, and his prayer was answered.

The weather itself was astonishing—blue snow coming down day after day, covering everything with its beauty. Suddenly a fierce storm arose; even mighty Paul had to wait a bit before venturing into it. But one day he did, and that is when he had a most strange experience.

This all happened quite a number of years ago, and by now the reports are just a little fuzzy. But no matter, the end result is what counts, and here is what took place.

While he was walking in the delightful blue snow, Paul tripped over something. Suddenly he heard a mooing sound. Curiosity caught him. He had to take a closer look. What he saw, of all things, were two enormous, hairy ears poking through the snowdrifts! Not only were they big and hairy, they were blue!

This was incredible.

"What is this? Who are you?" Paul wanted to know.

But there wasn't an answer. So Paul reached into the blue snow and pulled the ears. What should come out of the snow, but a baby ox! It was almost all blue—the body, the tail, the eyes. Only the nose was different. It was black. Besides being very blue, this was the largest calf Paul had ever seen. He could tell, for he felt his own muscles quiver when he lifted it. But the baby ox seemed more dead than alive, and Paul rushed it home to cover it with blankets. All night he tended the blue calf. At last, when dawn came, the ox suddenly stood up

and licked Paul's neck with his wet tongue, which tickled.

Paul laughed and shouted, "Babe, we'll be wonderful friends!"

Paul and Babe were soon working together in the logging business, with Paul chopping and Babe hauling.

The Blue Ox grew to an enormous size. There were no scales around to weigh Babe, but one day Paul measured the distance be-

tween Babe's eyes. That came to forty-two axe handles and one plug of chewing gum. Everyone agrees to that. Oh, it was a beautiful friendship. There wasn't anything the two couldn't work out together, no matter how tough the problem.

One of the problems for Paul was that Babe had an enormous appetite. Of course, large appetites were nothing new to Paul Bunyan. There was, after all, his own to contend with. He had his favorite foods, such as corn and flapjacks. Once while Paul was roaming the woods, he wandered into a lumber camp in Michigan. There he made friends with the cook, and a good thing, too, for Paul was quite hungry after his trek.

The cook put his twenty-two helpers to the task of feeding this giant of a lumberjack. It took the crew three hours to fix a meal worthy of his appetite. If this account of the menu had been passed down by word of mouth through the years, it might seem somewhat exaggerated. As it is, the list of food Paul ate comes straight from the cook's own records, so there can be no mistake about it.

The order in which he ate these foods probably doesn't matter. It didn't to Paul.

"I'm one hungry fella," he announced, and then he began.

According to the cook, this is what it took to satisfy Paul: two bushels of fried potatoes, thirty pounds of beef, half a dozen hams, one dozen extremely heavy loaves of bread, twelve

dozen eggs, 678 pancakes topped off with six gallons of syrup—and all this was washed down with approximately seven gallons of coffee.

That was a rather unusual day, to be sure, considering Paul had walked a long distance. But even on other days, when he wasn't quite as hungry, the dinner-table menu was still rather staggering. Or it would be for an ordinary person.

Paul recalls a time, though, when he actually did not finish his dinner. There was a reason for this! There had been a corn roast in the

camp, when suddenly the temperature changed drastically. It got so hot that the corn began popping, and soon the situation turned into a calamity. The corn piled in drifts, covering the cookhouse and living quarters. It frightened the birds, who thought it was winter and took off for the south. It is said that even Babe the Blue Ox turned bluer, because he thought snow was falling.

What was there to do but eat the popcorn?
The other lumberjacks ate and ate, and so did
Paul. Soon the men—their stomachs filled—
were shoveling popcorn into Paul's mouth. Finally the popcorn was gone. And Paul's appetite had dwindled.

"I'm kind of stuffed," he said. And then he
sat down to just a few bowls of soup, two or
three roast chickens—it's not certain quite how
many—six steaks with beans, squash, and
potatoes . . . followed by several stacks of pan-

cakes, a dozen donuts, an apple pie, bread and butter, and coffee, too. But that was all he could handle that day.

So when Paul decided, as he did, that he must have his own logging camp, you can see that food was something to think about very seriously.

Paul's first camp was on the Onion River, in the North Woods, perhaps up around Wisconsin or Michigan or Minnesota. This was Paul's dream come true.

To start, he hired a foreman, Hals Halvorsen, and a bookkeeper, Johnny Inkslinger. He hired a chief cook, Sourdough Sam. Then he hired another cook, Hot Biscuit Slim. Next he hired a blacksmith, Ole the Big Swede. And then came several hundred ordinary lumberjacks. His plan was to have the biggest logging camp ever, and in all likelihood that's just what he did have.

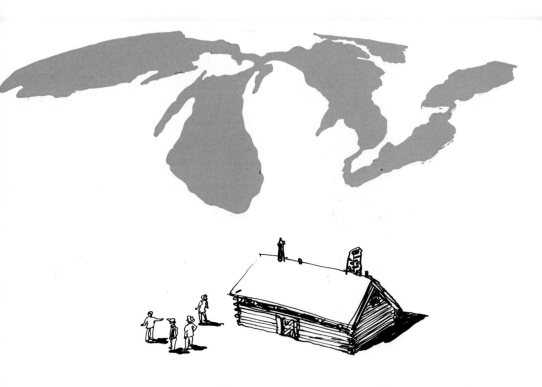

Paul had learned his geography well. He realized for such a huge camp he would need plenty of water, so—according to some stories—he dug the Great Lakes. Now, that might be taken with a grain of salt, for there is evidence that some mighty big lakes already did exist when he decided to start his camp. In any event, one way or another, Paul made certain he had a great supply of water. To get it to camp, he called on Babe, who regularly hauled the water in a huge tank.

Paul's first camp was so large that the men needed compasses and maps to get around. Some got lost, and despite the efforts of search parties, a few were never found.

The all-important cookhouse covered a four-square-mile area. It served all manner of excellent food. Moose and chicken stews were delicious, but the loggers' favorite was always

pancakes—the more the better. In fact, Paul had to drain a small lake so the cooks could have enough space to mix the batter. To grease the griddle, a number of kitchen helpers would tie slabs of bacon on their feet and skate over it. Then waiters would ride bicycles to the tables to serve the men. A pipeline brought syrup right to the tables, too.

"My lumberjacks love their hotcakes. Why make them wait?" reasoned Paul. Who will ever know how many flapjacks they ate at a sitting! And you can be sure that Paul ate as many as all the men put together, maybe even more.

This was the start of Paul's greatest logging adventures. The camp was a huge success. The loggers worked three shifts, around the clock, and millions of logs were cut. But Paul always replaced the cut trees with new seedlings.

There probably was little of this country that
Paul didn't see, or few places he didn't work.
He worked in the Dakotas, Oregon, and
Washington, besides working in the North
Woods. Wherever there was a tree—that was
Paul's business.

Moving on to new areas never was too dif-
ficult. The men simply loaded their equipment
in wagons, while Ole the Blacksmith placed
wheels under the dining room, the kitchen,
and the bunkhouses. Then Paul roped them
together with big chains, and Babe the Blue
Ox went to work, pulling the whole kaboodle
like so much straw!

If that sounds like some kind of a special feat for Babe—well, it's not so. There was a time, for instance, during logging days in Wisconsin, when Paul had to use a road so crooked that it couldn't find its own way through the forest. It was such a tangle that loggers starting home for camp would meet themselves coming back. There was only one thing to do. Paul hitched Babe to the end of

the road, then stood back and encouraged the big Blue Ox to pull.

"You can do it, Babe!" he cried. And how that ox strained and yanked and grunted. Then there came a deafening CRACK, and the road gave in to the mighty Babe. When everything quieted down, there was the road—perfectly straight.

How like his master Babe was. What endurance and strength! Of course, Paul did have special abilities. He was a man of the forests, a logger supreme, with a special understanding of the ways of all nature's creatures. It has been said, and there is no reason to disbelieve it, that Paul Bunyan was by far the best logger, hunter, fisherman, tracker, runner, mountain climber, log roller, and yeller. He was master of all kinds of outdoor activities. Evidence of that fact is everywhere.

And, of course, Paul was very good at problem-solving, which is what led to many of his inventions. Some of them somehow have become lost in the dust of time. Others are incorrectly said to be the work of more famous inventors. But the stories tell, and the records clearly show, that Paul was the source of many important inventions.

Take the simple donut—the donut was Paul's doing. One day he noticed that a cauldron of sourdough had boiled over. The cook was upset. But when the pot was removed, there sat a roll of dough with a hole in it. Paul gazed at it thoughtfully, then pried it loose and tossed it to his men.

"Thanks, Paul," they called back. "It's wonderful. What an idea!"

43

So the donut was born. And it's still everyone's favorite.

Paul also invented the grindstone and a chain axe that lopped off four trees at once. He designed a steam shovel to dig up vegetables. This was necessary because Paul grew vegetables of such a size that mere hand-digging would not work.

There have been numerous other accomplishments linked to Paul. For one thing, he tamed many periods of dreaded weather, sparing the lives of thousands. He straightened the Round River—no mean feat. It is said that he dug the St. Lawrence River, for a handsome price, to be sure. He freed the Yellowstone River from the Missouri River where they had become frozen together.

Paul also caused the Rocky Mountains and the Appalachian Mountains to form. While he was digging a canal in the middle of the country to float logs, dirt flew violently to the right and to the left. The Rockies grew on one side and the Appalachians on the other. When the

canal was done, Babe kicked over a bucket of water. And the canal was named the Mississippi. At least, that's what some of the tales tell. If it concerned the outdoors, you can just about be certain that Paul had something to do with it!

And now you wonder—what ever happened to Paul Bunyan? Has he gone, disappeared? Has he faded into a chapter of a storybook? Is he just a legend? Someone the young people and old-timers talk about from time to time?

The answer is—no matter what you think—Paul Bunyan, the master woodsman of all time, is still with us. There are a few loggers who still remember him well. They knew him, worked with him, and talked with him. They shared adventures from one corner of America to the other.

So if one day you should hear the cry *"Timber!"*, or hear the wind whistle in the trees, or feel a strange and sudden breeze, don't be surprised at what you might see. It could be Paul Bunyan—just around the bend.